PUFFIN BOOKS
THE CHERRY TREE

Born in Kasauli (Himachal Pradesh) in 1934, Ruskin Bond grew up in Jamnagar (Gujarat), Dehradun, New Delhi and Simla. His first novel *The Room on the Roof,* written when he was seventeen, received the John Llewellyn Rhys Memorial Prize in 1957. Since then he has written over five hundred short stories, essays and novellas (some included in the collections *Dust on the Mountains* and *Classic Ruskin Bond*) and more than forty books for children. He received the Sahitya Akademi Award for English writing in India in 1993, the Padma Shri in 1999, and the Delhi government's Lifetime Achievement Award in 2012. He has now been awarded the Sahitya Akademi's Bal Sahitya Puraskar for his 'total contribution to children's literature'.

He lives in Landour, Mussoorie, with his extended family.

D1416023

ALSO IN PUFFIN BY RUSKIN BOND

RUSKIN BOND

The Cherry Tree

Illustrated by
Manoj A. Menon

PUFFIN BOOKS

PUFFIN BOOKS

USA | Canada | UK | Ireland | Australia
New Zealand | India | South Africa | China

Puffin Books is part of the Penguin Random House group of companies
whose addresses can be found at global.penguinrandomhouse.com

Published by Penguin Random House India Pvt. Ltd
7th Floor, Infinity Tower C, DLF Cyber City,
Gurgaon 122 002, Haryana, India

Penguin
Random House
India

First published by Hamish Hamilton in the UK 1980
First published in India in Puffin by Penguin Books 2012

Text copyright @ Ruskin Bond 1980
Illustrations copyright @ Manoj A. Menon 2012

Book design by Bhavi Mehta

All rights reserved

14 13 12 11

ISBN 9780143332459

Typeset in Sabon
Printed at Replika Press Pvt. Ltd, India

www.penguin.co.in

One day, when Rakesh was six, he walked home from the Mussoorie bazaar eating cherries. They were a little sweet, a little sour; small, bright red cherries that had come all the way from the Kashmir Valley.

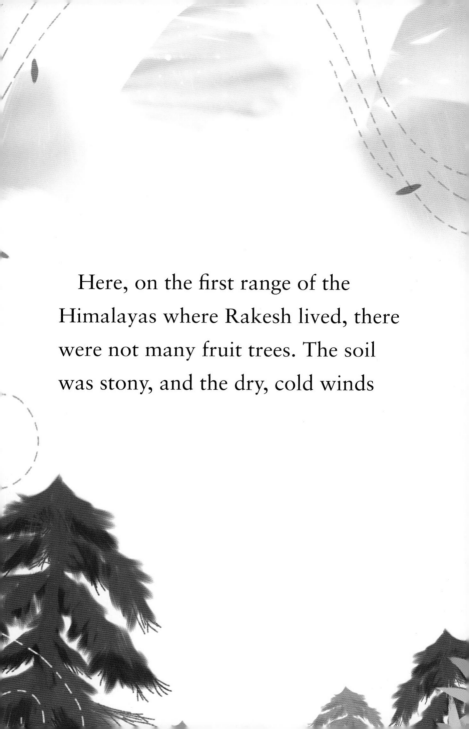

Here, on the first range of the Himalayas where Rakesh lived, there were not many fruit trees. The soil was stony, and the dry, cold winds stunted the growth of most plants. But on the more sheltered slopes there were forests of oak, maple and deodar.

Rakesh lived with his grandfather on the outskirts of the town, just where the forest began. His father and mother lived in a small village fifty miles away. Here they grew maize and rice and barley in narrow terraced fields on the lower slopes of the mountain. But there were no schools in their village. So as soon as Rakesh was old enough to go to school, his parents sent him to stay with his grandfather in the small town of Mussoorie.

Grandfather was a retired forest ranger. He had a little cottage outside the town.

Rakesh was on his way home from school when he bought the cherries, and by the time he reached the cottage there were only three left.

'Will you have a cherry, Dada?' he asked, as soon as he saw his grandfather in the garden.

Grandfather took one cherry and Rakesh promptly ate the other two.

He kept the last seed in his mouth for some time, rolling it round and round on his tongue until all the tang had gone. Then he placed the seed on the palm of his hand and studied it.

'Are cherry seeds lucky, Dada?' asked Rakesh.

'Of course.'

'Then I'll keep it.'

'Nothing is lucky if you put it away. If you want luck, you must put the seed to work.'

'How can I make it work?'

'Plant it.'

So Rakesh went to a corner of the garden where the earth was soft and yielding. He did not have to dig. He pressed the seed into the soil with his thumb and it went right in.

Then he had his lunch and ran off to play cricket with his friends, and forgot all about the cherry tree.

It was then mid-August, when the monsoon rains are at their heaviest, and plants spring up almost everywhere—from cracks in the walls of houses, from blocked drainpipes, and sometimes from the trunks of trees—and seeds and seedlings need no looking after . . .

When it was winter in the Himalayas, a cold wind blew down from the snows and wailed in the deodar trees.

All December and January the garden was dry and bare. The thick monsoon foliage had long since disappeared.

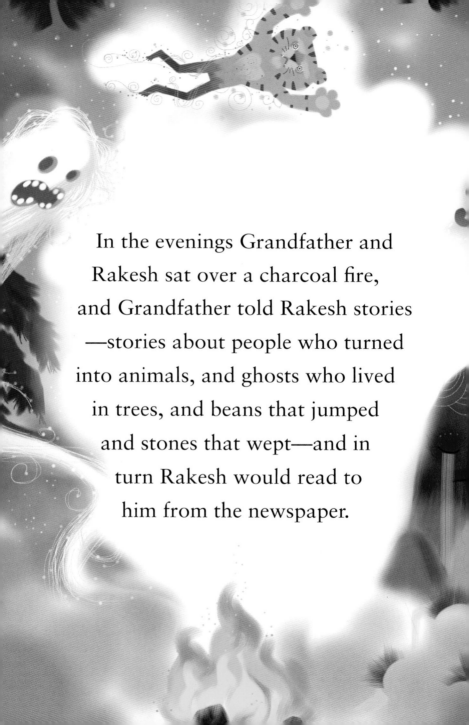

In the evenings Grandfather and Rakesh sat over a charcoal fire, and Grandfather told Rakesh stories —stories about people who turned into animals, and ghosts who lived in trees, and beans that jumped and stones that wept—and in turn Rakesh would read to him from the newspaper.

They knew it was spring when the ducks flew north again, to Siberia. Early in the morning when he got up to chop wood and light a fire, Rakesh saw the V-shaped formation of ducks streaming northwards, the calls of the

birds carrying clearly on the thin mountain air.

One morning in the garden, he bent to pick up what he thought was a small twig and found to his surprise that it was well rooted. He stared at it for a moment, then ran to fetch Grandfather, calling, 'Dada, come and look, the cherry tree has come up!'

'What cherry tree?' asked Grandfather, who had forgotten about it.

'The seed we planted last year—look, it's come up!'

Rakesh went on his knees, while Grandfather bent double and peered down at the tiny tree. It was about four inches high.

'Yes, it's a cherry tree all right,' said Grandfather. 'You must water it now and then.'

Rakesh watered it and circled it with pebbles.

'What are the pebbles for?' asked Grandfather.

'For privacy,' replied Rakesh.

He looked at the tree every morning, but it did not seem to be growing very fast. So he stopped looking at it— except quickly, out of the corner of his eye. And after a week or two, when he allowed himself to look at it properly, he found that it *had* grown—at least an inch!

That year the monsoon rains came early, and Rakesh plodded to and from school in his raincoat and gumboots. Ferns grew from the rocks, strange-looking lilies came up in the long grass, and even when it wasn't raining, the trees dripped and mist came curling up the valley. The cherry tree grew quickly in this season.

When the tree was about two feet high, a goat entered the garden and ate all the young leaves. Rakesh spotted the goat as he was coming down the path. He chased it out of the garden and all the way down the hill until it leapt across a small ravine. But when he returned to the garden, out of breath and still very angry, he found that only the cherry tree's main stem and two thin branches remained.

'Never mind,' consoled Grandfather, seeing that Rakesh was upset. 'It will grow again; cherry trees are tough.'

Towards the end of the rainy season new leaves appeared on the tree. And then one day a woman cutting grass came scrambling down the hillside, her scythe swishing through everything that came in the way. One sweep, and the cherry tree was cut in two.

Grandfather saw what had happened. He went up to the woman and scolded her.

'What do you mean by cutting our tree?' he demanded.

'I didn't see it,' answered the woman. 'I was cutting the grass.'

'You weren't looking,' said Grandfather. 'And anyway, who asked you to cut our grass?'

'It was long. It needed cutting. I'm taking it home for my cows!'

'You won't cut any of our grass without my permission,' fumed Grandfather. 'And besides, I like long grass. I like looking at it. I like walking on it. I like sitting on it.'

The woman went away muttering something about the old man being crazy. Grandfather bent over the cherry tree and examined it closely; it looked as though the damage could not be repaired.

'Maybe it will die now,' said Rakesh, looking downcast.

'Maybe,' agreed Grandfather.

The cherry tree had no intention
of dying.

By the time summer came round
again, it had sent out several new shoots
with tender green leaves. Rakesh had
grown taller, too. He was eight now,
a sturdy boy with curly black hair and
deep black eyes. 'Blackberry eyes,'
Grandfather called them. They were
like the wild blackberries growing
on the hillside.

The berries ripened in July. Rakesh
collected a bagful of them, and
Grandfather made blackberry jam—
three jars, which lasted through
the summer.

Another monsoon came and went, and during it Rakesh went home to his village, to help his father and mother with the ploughing and sowing and planting. He was thinner but stronger when he came back to Grandfather's house at the end of the rains. He found that the cherry tree had grown another foot. It was now up to his chest.

Even when there was plenty of rain,
Rakesh would sometimes water the
tree. He wanted it to know that he
was *there*.

One day he found a bright green
praying mantis perched on a branch,
peering at him with bulging eyes. It
was the cherry tree's first visitor. It
would not harm the tree. On the
contrary, it was soon busy snapping
up all the leaf-cutting insects that
came its way.

Next day there was another visitor—
a hairy caterpillar who started making a
meal of several leaves. Rakesh removed
it quickly and dropped it over the wall.
He had learnt at school about ugly

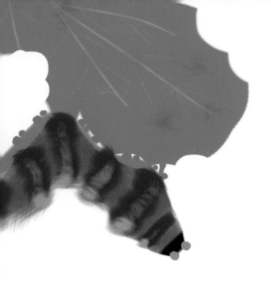

caterpillars turning into beautiful
butterflies, so he didn't want to kill it;
nor did he want it eating up all the leaves.

He watched the caterpillar crawl away
and said, 'Come back when you're
a butterfly.'

Winter came early that year. The cherry tree bent low with the weight of snow. Field mice sought shelter in the roof of the cottage. The road to Mussoorie was blocked by snow, and for several days there was no newspaper. This made Grandfather quite grumpy. His stories began to have unhappy endings.

'This won't do,' he said to himself. 'Nobody loves a sad man.' And so to cheer himself and Rakesh he began singing merry songs, and kept singing until the weather cleared.

In February it was Rakesh's birthday.

He was nine—and the tree was four, but almost as tall as Rakesh. They had a tea party in the garden. Grandfather was good at tea parties. Rakesh's friends came and ate up everything there was to eat. Then they sang and danced round the cherry tree and played hide-and-seek on the hillside until it grew dark.

One morning when the sun came out, Grandfather came into the garden to 'let some warmth into my bones' as he put it. He stopped in front of the cherry tree, stared at it for a few seconds, and then called out, 'Rakesh! Come and look! Quickly, before it falls!'

Rakesh dashed outside, wondering if the house was falling down. He found Grandfather staring at the tree as if it had performed a miracle. There was a pale pink blossom at the end of a branch.

The seasons passed, turning the forest from light green to dark green to red to brown to gold, and in the following year there were more blossoms. And then the tree was taller than Rakesh, even though it was less than half his age. And then it was taller than Grandfather, who was older than some of the oak and maple trees.

Rakesh had grown too. He could run

and jump and climb trees better than most boys. He read a lot of books too, although he still liked listening to Grandfather's tales.

In the cherry tree, bees came to feed on the nectar, and tiny birds pecked at the blossoms and broke them off. But the tree kept flowering right through the spring, and there were always more blossoms than birds.

That summer there were small cherries on the tree. Rakesh tasted one and spat it out.

'It's too sour,' he said.

'They'll be better next year,' said Grandfather.

But the birds liked them. Yellow-bottomed bulbuls and scarlet minivets flitted in and out of the foliage, feasting on the sour cherries.

On a warm, sunny afternoon, when even the bees seemed drowsy, Rakesh looked out of the bedroom window and saw Grandfather reclining on a cane chair under the cherry tree. It was the first time Grandfather had taken his easy chair into the garden.

'There's just the right amount of shade here,' he said. 'And I like looking up at the leaves.'

'They're bright shiny leaves,' said

Rakesh. 'And they spin like tops when there's a breeze.'

After Grandfather had gone indoors, Rakesh came into the garden and began weeding the flower beds. When he was tired he lay down on the grass beneath the cherry tree. He gazed up through the leaves at the great blue sky; and turning on his side, he could see the mountain striding away into the clouds. He was still lying beneath the tree when the evening shadows crept across the garden.

Grandfather came back and sat down beside Rakesh. They waited in silence until the stars came out and the nightjar began to call. In the forest below, the crickets and cicadas began shrilling and squeaking like an orchestra tuning up; then they all started playing together, and the trees were filled with the sound of insects.

'So many trees in the forest,' mused Rakesh. 'Why do I like this one so much?'

'You planted it yourself,' said Grandfather. 'That's why it's special.'

Rakesh touched the smooth bark of the tree. He ran his hand along the

trunk and put his finger to the
tip of a leaf. He reached up and
was just able to touch the
highest branch.

'Over six feet tall,' he said.
'Tall, strong cherry tree, all
grown by me!'

Read More in Puffin

Getting Granny's Glasses

by Ruskin Bond

Mani's Granny is seventy and can barely see through her old, scratched glasses. With only a hundred and fifty rupees in their pocket and a thirst for adventure, Mani and Granny set off to buy a new pair. On the way, they get drenched in heavy showers, run into mules and encounter a terrible landslide. Will Granny ever be able to reach the town and get herself a new pair of glasses?

This beautifully illustrated edition brings alive the magical charm of one of Ruskin Bond's most unforgettable tales.